P9-ELS-771

DREAMWORKS

MADAGASCAR 2

ESCAPE 2 AFRICA

WRITTEN BY LOKI

ILLUSTRATED BY MADA DESIGN, INC.

MEREDITH® BOOKS

DES MOINES, IOWA

Alex, Marty, Melman, and Gloria are finally heading home to New York City on Air Penguin. King Julien throws a wild party to say goodbye to his favorite pansies as they leave Madagascar.

Find these things:

When Air Penguin crash lands in Africa, the penguins need to find parts to fix the plane. They trick some tourists and take their truck for spare parts. Unfortunately one of those tourists is Nana—watch out, Alex!

Find these things:

MAP

Alex, Marty, Melman, and Gloria look out over the African horizon in awe. Alex finds this new land strangely familiar. As they approach the water hole, the four friends come face-to-face with animals just like themselves for the very first time.

Find these things:

Zuba and Florrie recognize Alex as their long-lost son, Alakay. Zuba, the king of the lions, calls for a festive pool party. But one lion, Makunga, doesn't feel like celebrating.

Find these things:

Alex soon learns that to be a member of the lion pride, he must pass a test. But he thinks the test is a dance-off. Unfortunately Alex's opponent, Teetsi, is ready to fight, not dance.

Find these things:

When Alex loses the fight, he is banished from the pride. Alex is so embarrassed, he just wants to go home. But with the monkeys on strike, it doesn't look like the plane will be ready anytime soon.

Find these things:

Then the water hole dries up, and King Julien talks Melman into being a sacrifice to the volcano! But Gloria decides that she loves the big lug as much as he loves her, and she saves him at the last minute.

Find these things:

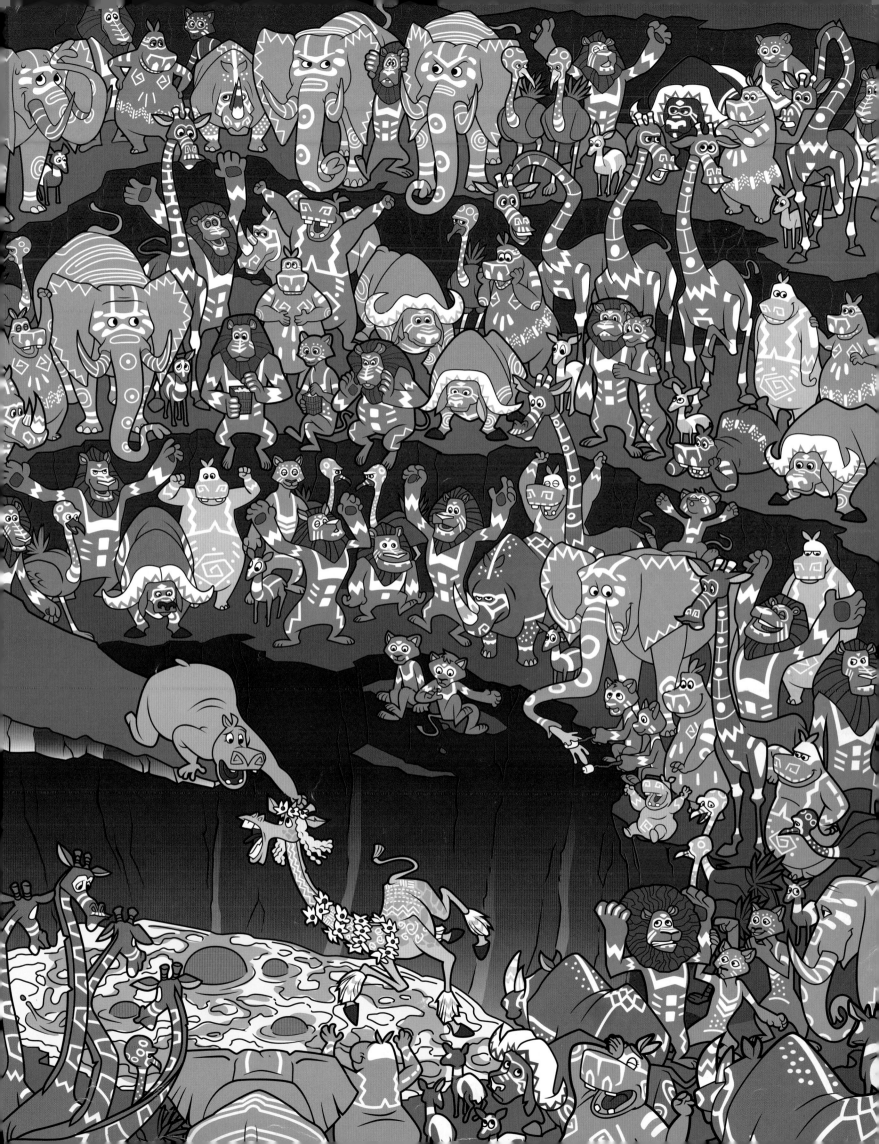

Alex wants to earn Zuba's respect by fixing the water hole. When Alex dances his way out of trouble with Nana's nutty tribe, his dad finally understands his unique talents.

Find these things:

The penguin-piloted plane
and a chain of monkeys
swing by, and Alex and Zuba
jump onboard. Alex sees
the perfect opportunity to
destroy Nana's dam and
fix the water hole. He and
Zuba just need to hold on
tight. Woosh!

Find these things:

KRW 122

0293 TB
LAB 91-92
9632 ARG

As water gushes back into the water hole, the celebration begins. Zuba is king again; Alex is a member of the pride; Gloria loves Melman; and they all move it, move it to the music!

Find these things: